Stories for 2 year-olds

BONNEY PRESS

Contents

Published by Bonney Press
an imprint of Hinkler Books Pty Ltd
45–55 Fairchild Street
Heatherton Victoria 3202 Australia
www.hinkler.com

BONNEY
PRESS

© Hinkler Books Pty Ltd 2019

Authors: Annaliese Stoney, Melissa Mattox, Helen O'Dare
Illustrators: Annaliese Stoney, Irisz Agócs, Nicola O'Byrne, Marie Simpson
Design: Aimee Forde
Prepress: Splitting Image

ISBN: 978 1 4889 1447 8

Printed and bound in China

Welcome to
Stories for 2-year-olds

Storytime can be the snuggliest part of the day
with your 2-year-old—and a good storybook can ignite your child's
imagination and teach them lots about the world, and themselves!

Reading together is also one of the best things you can do for your toddler's
development! Did you know that by age two, most children can use up to
50 words and understand an amazing 75 to 225 words, along with simple
sentences? And by the time they turn three, almost everything they say will
be understandable. This really is a great period to encourage your child's
language development! Reading aloud will help your toddler become familiar
with words, sounds, and handling books, smoothing the transition to
independent reading and learning later on.

Stories for 2-year-olds contains three perfect stories to enjoy
with your child—especially chosen to be accessible and engaging
for 2-year-olds. We've also included a fun nursery rhyme
to round out the collection!

It's Not JUST a Blanket is a fabulously funny tale that many toddlers will identify with, about creative play and a comfort blanket. The hilarious illustrations by Annaliese Stoney will have everyone giggling!

The Best Ballerina is a sweet story about three animal friends who can't decide who gets to wear the perfect fairy-princess costume for the ballet recital. Will the show be ruined, or can the girls work together to create true fairy-princess magic? Your child will love the uplifting message about friendship.

Finally, the bestselling classic *Love* explores the joys of unconditional love between a parent and child. With evocative illustrations by Nicola O'Byrne and a captivating rhyming story, this is the perfect choice for soothing your little one to sleep.

Happy reading!

It's not JUST a blanket!

Written and illustrated by
ANNALIESE STONEY

BONNEY PRESS

For Steve and my family,
for all their cheerleading!

Sophia *loved* her blanket **VERY** much.

Everywhere...

and

ANYWHERE

that she and her dog Monty went,

the blanket came too!

Her family didn't understand why.

"It's *JUST* a blanket!"

they said.

But Sophia knew better.

"It's not *JUST* a blanket. It's a..."

Wriggly Worm!

MUNCH
MUNCH

It's not JUST a blanket!

It's a...

Slippery stingray!

It's not JUST a blanket! It's a...

15

PIRATE SHIP!

It's not JUST a blanket! look! It's a...

MAGIC CARPET

And it's not JUST a blanket! It's a...

19

And it's not **JUST** a blanket! It's a...

SNOOZING

BAT!

In fact, because it's not **JUST** a blanket, it's worth...

Poor Sophia was very upset.

Monty felt pretty bad, too.

Her brother Clive saw the whole thing.

He told the whole family,

who thought very hard, until eventually they came up with

A BRILLIANT PLAN...

$mc^2 = \frac{1}{4}$

First, Dad collected all
the torn bits of blanket.

Clive took off his starry socks.

Grandma found an old pair of bloomers,

and Mom generously donated Dad's Hawaiian shirt collection.

Then, armed with a big bundle of material, they worked very, very hard, until...

GASP!

"TA-DA!" they exclaimed.
"Here you are Sophia and Monty. We know how much you
loved that old blanket, so we've made you BOTH new blankets."

"Thank you very much!" Sophia and Monty said.

"The only thing is...

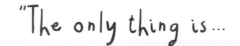

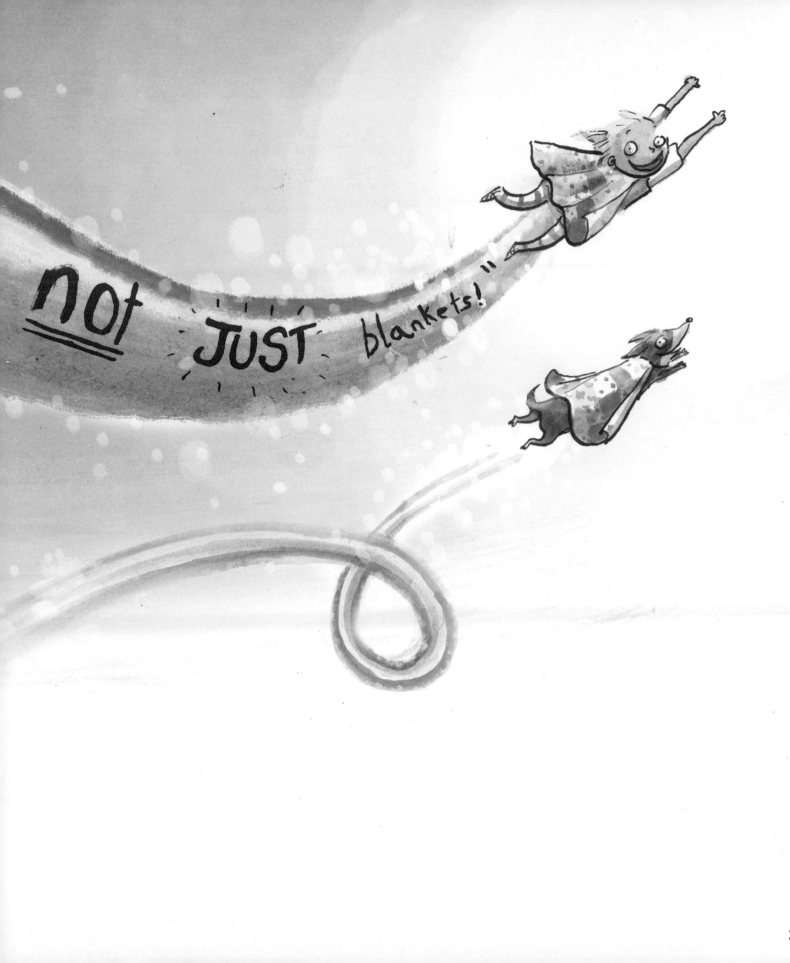

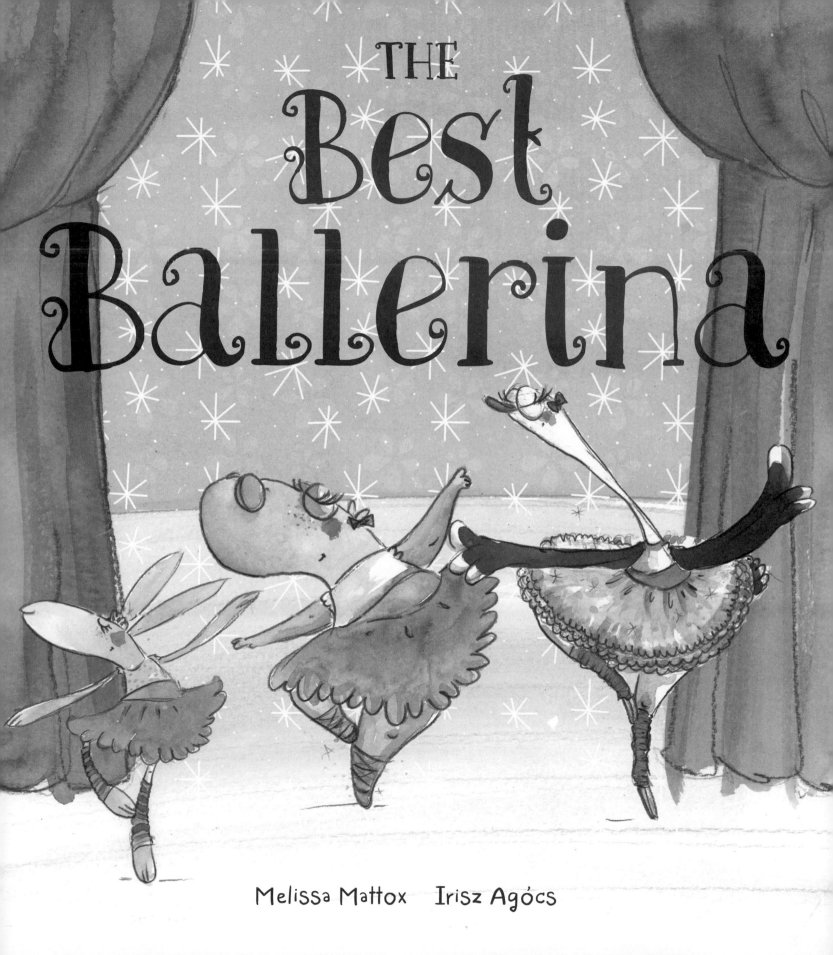

THE Best Ballerina

Melissa Mattox   Irisz Agócs

Harriet was so excited. She wanted to show her friends her new ballet slippers.

"Those are beautiful! And they match my tutu perfectly," said Olivia. "Together they will make a perfect fairy-princess costume."

"Not without this, they don't!" said Rachel.

"Ooooh," hummed the girls, happily.

The three friends twirled and spun, leaped, and pirouetted.

As they danced, all they could think about was the upcoming big ballet recital.

"Oh no! I just realized something," said Harriet, stopping mid-dance. "We only have enough pieces for one fairy-princess costume.

Only one of us can dance in the big ballet recital!"

"Well, it should be me," said Olivia.
"I have the longest legs."

"But I brought the tiara!" interrupted Rachel.

"That shouldn't matter!"
cried Harriet.

Each girl tried on the costume.

But no matter how hard they tried, it just didn't look right.

The friends continued to argue, each one convinced that she was the best fairy-princess dancer.

"Ladies, why all the fussing?" asked Madam Hoot.

Harriet, Olivia, and Rachel explained the problem.

Madam Hoot listened carefully.

"The night sky is never lit by just one star but shines because there are many," she said. "Why don't you three get some rest? Tomorrow you can choose who should wear the costume at the recital."

That night the girls lay in their beds, staring up at the dark night sky, all lit up with hundreds of twinkling starry lights.

The next morning, the three friends met before the dance.

"I'm sorry we fought," said Rachel. "I think Harriet should dance. She has the best twirls."

"But Olivia has the best pliés," said Harriet.

"No one can beat Rachel's leaps,"
offered Olivia.

A crowd had gathered to watch the girls perform.
"Bravo!" "Hooray!" "Magnificent!" they shouted.

"I think the best fairy princess for the big ballet recital should be... all three of us!" said Olivia. "Together we make true fairy-princess magic!"

Love

Helen O'Dare

Nicola O'Byrne

Love

can be **gigantic** like a **mountain**,
and **small** and **precious** like a **diamond**.

Love

stretches up, up, **tall** like a **tree**,
but secured by its **roots** so **deep**.

Love

has **wings** that help you **fly**
above the **clouds** in the **big blue sky**.

Love

is there in a **tickle** and a **giggle**
and an **enormous** belly-laugh **wiggle!**

Love
can be **loud** like a trumpet's **blares**
that sometimes **catch** you **unawares!**

Love

is a **book** and a **warm** milk mug,
and makes the **rainy** days all **snug**.

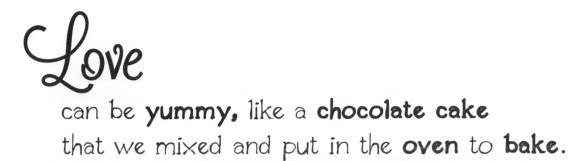

Love

can be **yummy,** like a **chocolate cake**
that we mixed and put in the **oven** to **bake.**

Love
can make you **sing** out **loud.**
You always make me feel so **proud!**

Love

can be **splashes** and **soap** and **bubbles**.
I will always **love** your **cuddles**!

Love

is **strong** and **true** like a **big bear hug**
that you give to a **sleepy** little **snuggle-bug**.

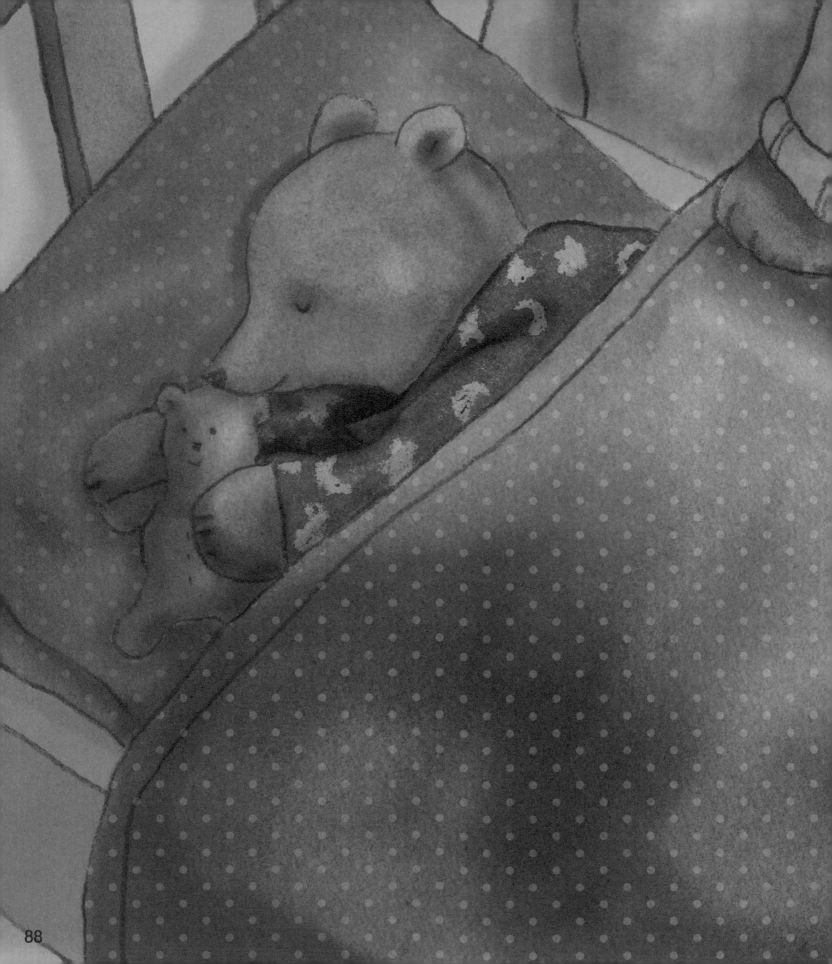

Love

is **big** and **wide**
and **ocean deep.**
It's even **there**
when you're **asleep.**

Love
is all of these, it's true.
And that's how much **I love YOU!**

Teddy Bear, Teddy Bear

Teddy bear, teddy bear, turn around;

Teddy bear, teddy bear, touch the ground.

Teddy bear, teddy bear, climb the stairs;

Teddy bear, teddy bear, say your prayers.

Teddy bear, teddy bear, turn out the light;

Teddy bear, teddy bear, say goodnight!

Goodnight!